The Two Foolish Cats

Yoshiko Uchida
The Two Foolish Cats
Suggested by a Japanese folktale

illustrated by Margot Zemach

Margaret K. McElderry Books
NEW YORK

Suggested by the Japanese folktale
Saru No Nigirimeshi Saiban

Text copyright © 1987 by Yoshiko Uchida
Illustrations copyright © 1987 by Margot Zemach

Margaret K. McElderry Books
Macmillan Publishing Company
866 Third Avenue
New York, N.Y. 10022
Collier Macmillan Canada, Inc.

Composition by Linoprint Composition
New York, New York
Printed and bound in Hong Kong by Toppan Printing Company

10   9   8   7   6   5   4   3   2   1
First edition

12/87

Library of Congress Cataloging-in-Publication Data
Uchida, Yoshiko.
The two foolish cats.

Summary: Two foolish cats go to the old monkey of the
mountain to settle their quarrel.
[1. Folklore—Japan.   2. Cats—Folklore]   I. Zemach,
Margot, ill.   II. Title.   III. Title: 2 foolish cats.
PZ8.1.U35Tw   1987   398.2'452974428'0952   [E]   86-12660
ISBN 0-689-50397-0

For Gordon and Ruri

Y.U.

For Bobbi and Aviva

M.Z.

Long ago, at the edge of a dark pine forest in Japan, there lived two cats named Daizo and Suki. Because Daizo was big and fierce and had seven toes on each paw, he was called Big Daizo. Because Suki was small and skinny, he was called Little Suki.

When the field mice saw Big Daizo swishing his tail and stalking through the tall grass, they ran to hide in their tiny holes. They were afraid of Big Daizo, for they knew he could pounce on them with his seven-toed paws and swallow them in one gulp for dinner.

The birds of the forest were afraid of Little Suki, for they knew that if he caught them, he would surely gobble them down in a minute.

The two cats got on quite well and hunted together each day in the meadows and streams. One spring morning when the snow had melted from the mountains and the meadows were turning green, they went out to catch some field mice for breakfast. They hunched low in the tall grass, waiting and watching, silent and still.

But the field mice saw the two cats waiting for them.

"Not for anything will we go out today," they whispered, and they huddled safe in their cozy nests.

Soon Little Suki grumbled, "Those field mice are never coming out. Let's go catch some fish instead."

So the two cats raced as fast as they could to the stream at the edge of the meadow.

Big Daizo plunged first into the icy waters. SPLATT! SPLASH! He pounced on a silvery trout. But the fish was much too fast for him. It shimmered and slipped away swiftly down the mountain stream.

"You are much too slow," Little Suki scoffed. "You must be quick and clever like me. Watch!"

And Little Suki jumped into the stream, his sharp claws spread, his whiskers twitching. SPLATT! SPLASH! He pounced, quick as lightning. But today, the speckled trout were too fast even for him.

"You're not so fast after all," Big Daizo complained. "You didn't catch a single fish."

"Well, neither did you," Little Suki hissed.

"Eowrrrrr," the cats growled, glaring at each other.

They sat at the edge of the stream, wet and hungry. Just when they had decided to give up and go home, they saw two rice cakes in the tall reeds nearby. One was big and plump, but the other was very small.

"Look!" Little Suki shouted. And because he was faster, he got to the rice cakes first.

"I'll take the big one," he said, "because I'm small and skinny and need more food to grow on."

"Oh no you don't!" Big Daizo hissed. "I should have the biggest rice cake because I need more food than you do. Give it to me at once!"

"No!" Little Suki shouted. "The big one is mine!"

"You are not only skinny and scrawny," Big Daizo screeched, "you are stubborn and greedy as well!"

Soon the two cats were snarling and spitting at each other. They clawed and scratched, they hissed and yowled, and they chased each other around and around the trees.

The field mice looked out from their holes and watched the cats fight.

"*Banzai*! Hooray!" they squealed. "Maybe they will eat each other up and leave us alone."

The blue jays and mockingbirds flew down to see what the racket was all about.

"Look! Look!" they cried. "The two cats are fighting. They are so greedy and stubborn, they will never stop."

Soon the old badger hurried out from the forest.

"Stop your yowling and screeching," he scolded. "You are making so much noise, you will awaken the Thunder God in the sky, and then he will tilt the rain barrels and pour rain on all our heads!"

Since Big Daizo and Little Suki were growing weary, they stopped snarling long enough to tell the badger about the two rice cakes.

"All that racket over two silly rice cakes?" the old badger asked. "Go find the old monkey of the mountain," he told the cats. "He is clever and wise and he will settle your quarrel. He will see that you get equal shares."

"That is a fine idea," the two cats agreed, for by now they wanted to stop fighting and eat their rice cakes.

So Big Daizo and Little Suki hurried through the pine forest, heading toward the mountain where the wise old monkey lived. They followed curving paths that wound through the trees. They climbed over logs and under curtains of moss. They crossed a marsh and scrambled through thick vines. Finally, they stopped for a drink at a deep mountain pool.

"Garrump...garrump..." the great frog who guarded the pool called out to them. "What brings you cats to my mountain pool?"

"We are going to see the wise old monkey of the mountain," they explained. "Tell us, are we almost there?"

"You must go up and up and around and over, and then up and up some more," the frog garrumped.

So the two cats hurried on. Up and up and around and over, and up and up some more.

At last they passed through a grove of bamboo and reached the top of the mountain. And there was the wise old monkey, sitting on a tree branch, having a cup of tea.

The two cats held up their rice cakes and both began to talk at once.

"Stop! One at a time!" the old monkey scolded.

So Big Daizo held up the small rice cake and told the monkey why he should have the big one. And Little Suki held up the big rice cake and told why he deserved to keep it.

"Ah *hah*, ah *hah*," the old monkey said, stroking his chin. "I see your problem and I will solve it for you."

"Thank you, Mr. Monkey," the two cats purred. "We knew you were wiser than anyone in the forest."

The old monkey disappeared into his house and soon returned with a pair of tiny scales. He put one rice cake on each side of the scale, but of course they did not balance.

"Ah *hah*, ha *hah*," the monkey said. "I can soon fix that."

And he quickly took a bite from the larger rice cake.

"Now," he said, "they should both be equal."

But he had eaten too much, and now the smaller rice cake was heavier.

"Ah *hah*, ha *hah*, I can soon fix that," the old monkey said. And this time he took a bite from the smaller rice cake.

But of course he had again eaten too much.

"Ah *hah*, ha *hah*, I shall soon fix that," the old monkey said once more, and he took still another bite.

"Ah...er...uh...Mr. Wise Monkey, sir," Big Daizo said, twitching his whiskers. "Don't you think you have taken quite enough from each rice cake?"

"Yes, yes," Little Suki agreed. "Surely they must be equal by now."

But the clever old monkey paid no attention to the cats. He just went right on, weighing and munching, weighing and munching, until at last he had eaten up both rice cakes.

Then he looked slyly at the two cats and said, "Well, your rice cakes are now equally gone. I told you I would stop your quarreling and indeed I have. For now there is nothing left for you to quarrel about."

And with a quick flick of his tail, the old monkey took his tiny scales and disappeared into his house.

"Eowrrr..." Big Daizo wailed. "I feel foolishly *stupid*."

And Little Suki wailed, "Eowrrr...I feel stupidly *foolish*."

Above their heads the blue jays laughed and the mockingbirds mocked, "Silleeeee cats! Fooooolish cats!" And they flew through the forest telling everyone the tale of the two foolish cats.

When the old badger heard them, he roared with laughter.

"Ha ha, ha ha!
   Ho ho, ho ho!
   What foolish cats!
   Their rice cakes are gone!"

When the mice in the meadow heard the tale, they scrambled out of their holes and danced with joy.

"Ha ha, ho ho,
   Ha ha, hee hee," they sang.
"The wise old monkey
   Fooled Daizo and Suki!"

As Big Daizo and Little Suki slunk home quietly, they heard the sounds of laughter echoing all through the forest and fields and far out into the starry skies.

And ever since that day, the two cats never quarreled again, but lived peacefully together at the edge of the dark pine forest.